The Sweet Shop Clean Up

Written by Jonny Walker
Illustrated by Richard Watson

OXFORD
UNIVERSITY PRESS

Ralf was waiting for a bus to take him into town.

He was off to work at the sweet shop, Sweet Treats.

Soon, the bus arrived.

'One return ticket into town, please,' Ralf said to the driver.

Ralf handed over a **coin**.

The bus set off.

What is the **value** of the **coin** in Ralf's hand?

It wasn't long before Ralf arrived at the sweet shop. The bell above the door jingled as he went in.

The air smelled sugary. There were jars full of sweets on the shelves.

The shopkeeper was called Mrs Bonbon.

'Hello, Ralf!' she said. 'Can you look after the shop for a while, please? I need to go to the bank.'

'Yes, of course,' Ralf replied.

What is the **value** of the **coin** in Mrs Bonbon's hand?

Ralf had never been in charge of the shop on his own before. He was so excited and nervous, his tummy felt like a fizzy sweet.

Ralf decided to clean the shop as a nice surprise for Mrs Bonbon.

Suddenly, the door swung open.

'Netty!' Ralf exclaimed.

'Hello, Ralf!' Netty replied. 'I'd like to buy some jelly beans, please.'

'That will be **one pound**, please,' Ralf said.

Look at the **coins** in Netty's hand. Point to the **coin** that is worth **one pound**. What other **coins** is Netty holding?

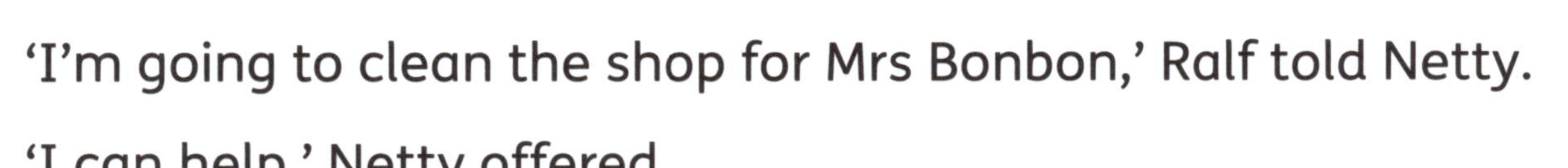

'I'm going to clean the shop for Mrs Bonbon,' Ralf told Netty.

'I can help,' Netty offered.

Ralf found the vacuum cleaner, but there was a problem. 'It's broken!' he said.

‘Don’t worry, Ralf,’ Netty said. ‘We can fix it. In fact, I think we can make it even better!’

Ralf grinned.

Ralf and Netty found a box of tools and some useful bits and pieces in the store cupboard. Together, they worked on the vacuum cleaner.

‘What shall we call it?’ Ralf asked, when they had finished.

‘How about … the Dream Clean Machine!’ Netty replied.

‘It can dust, vacuum, *and* mop!’ Ralf added proudly.

He tapped a button.

First, the Dream Clean Machine began to dust the jars on the shelves.

Then, the Dream Clean Machine began to vacuum the floor.

After that, the Dream Clean Machine began to mop, making the floor shine.

Just then, the Dream Clean Machine bumped into a pile of boxes. Lollipops spilled out everywhere.

The machine sped up. It began to dust, vacuum, and mop at the same time.

Before Ralf could turn off the machine, one of the mops hit the till. The drawer burst open.

Count the **coins**. How many **one pence coins** can you see? How many **ten pence coins** can you see? How many **five pence coins** can you see? What is the **total value** of each type of **coin**?

The machine began to suck up the **coins** in the till drawer!

'Oh, no!' Ralf shouted.

What is the **total value** of the **ten pence coins** being sucked up?
What is the **total value** of the **five pence coins** in the drawer?
What do you notice about the **total value** of the two sets of **coins**?

Netty switched off the machine.

'It's sucked up every single **coin**!' cried Ralf.

'Don't worry,' Netty said. 'We can get them out.'

Netty opened the vacuum cleaner and poured the **coins** out onto the floor.

‘There are three different types of **coin**,’ said Netty.

What are the three different types of **coin** in Netty’s hands?

Ralf and Netty worked together, sorting the **coins** into groups.

Then they put the **coins** back in the till.

What is the **total value** of the **coins** in each group?

Ralf sighed with relief, then looked at the shop. 'It's messier than it was before,' he said sadly.

'Let's clean it together,' Netty suggested.

This time, they didn't use a machine. They did it themselves.

They did a wonderful job. The sweet shop had never looked so clean. It made the sweets look even more tasty and delicious.

When Mrs Bonbon returned, she looked around the shop and grinned. 'What a great job you've done cleaning the shop,' she said. 'You can both have some sweets for free.'

Ralf picked some fizzy cherry sweets. Netty chose some chocolate buttons.

Ralf and Netty stepped out into the sunshine, holding their bags of sweets. It was time to go home.

Help Ralf in the sweet shop

What is the **total amount** of money in each box?

DRAGONS OF MOON TAIL ISLAND

Ember Saves the Day

Written by Maryann Wright
Illustrated by Lisa Hunt

OXFORD
UNIVERSITY PRESS

Meet the characters ...

Ember is a dragon from Moon Tail Island. Dragons can only be seen by those who truly believe in them.

Nadia and Omar are friends with Ember.

Dad

Nini, the children's gran

It was a sunny weekend and the family were going camping.

'We can make a den in the woods,' said Nadia.

'We can toast marshmallows!' exclaimed Omar.

'We can do that, and more!' said Nini.

Ember was looking forward to camping, too. Nadia had invited her to come along.

Ember sat on the workshop roof, waiting for them to set off.

Omar checked the weather forecast on Dad's phone. 'It says that there will be a big thunderstorm tonight,' he warned.

'I'm sure we'll be OK,' Dad said. 'The sky is so blue!'

Soon, they arrived at the campsite. They looked for a good place to set up camp.

'We need somewhere flat for the tent,' said Nini.

They all had fun working out how to put up the tent.

Omar and Nini held up the poles. Nadia helped Dad with the pegs.

Find these **3-D shapes** in the picture: **cuboid**, **cylinder**, **sphere**, **pyramid**, **triangular prism**. There might be more than one!

Once they were all set up, Nadia and Omar wanted to go and find Ember.

'Can we go off and explore?' asked Nadia.

'Sure, but don't wander off too far!' said Dad.

Find these **3-D shapes** in the picture:
cylinder, cuboid, cube, sphere, triangular prism.

They spotted Ember covered in leaves and twigs.

'There you are, Ember,' said Nadia. 'Great disguise!'

They all had fun exploring.

A little while later, Omar realized something important.

'Where are you going to sleep, Ember?' he asked. 'You don't have a tent. There's going to be a big storm!'

Nadia thought quickly. She looked around for ideas.

'Let's build you a den, Ember!' she said.

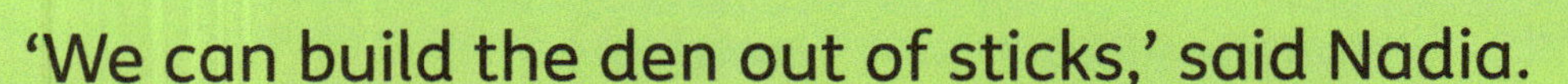

'We can build the den out of sticks,' said Nadia.

The children and Ember started to gather lots of sticks. Soon they had a big pile.

They used sticks to make a den. When it was done, Ember crawled inside. ‘It’s very cosy,’ she said.

What **3-D shape** does Ember’s den look like?

Later, back at their tent, the children helped Dad to make dinner.

'Let's sing some songs!' said Nini, after they had eaten.

They had great fun singing together.

Find these shapes in the picture:

2-D: hexagons, circles, triangles

3-D: cylinders, cubes, spheres

That night, Nadia woke up to the sound of rain drops on the tent. Soon, it was pouring down with rain.

The wind began to howl. The tents bent sideways. Thunder crashed and lightning flashed. Nadia peeked out of the tent door.

Omar was right. It was a big storm!

Meanwhile, in her den, Ember was also woken up by the thunder. She saw the tents getting blown about. Some of the tent pegs were coming loose. Suddenly, she had an idea.

Ember found some rocks and used them to weigh the tent pegs down.

However, there weren't enough rocks for all the pegs. Ember stretched out her wings to block the wind instead.

It helped to stop some of the tents flapping about.

Luckily the storm did not last for long. Thanks to Ember, everyone's tents stayed up.

'Well done, Ember!' said Nadia, when the children found out what Ember had done.

Later that morning, Dad and Nini looked around with confusion.

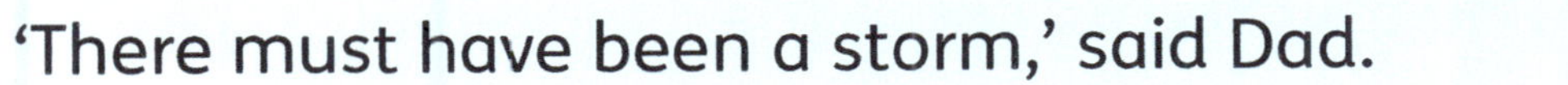

'There must have been a storm,' said Dad.

'I don't know how we slept through it!' said Nini.

What **2-D** and **3-D shapes** can you see?

The family had a wonderful day. First, they went on a bike ride. Then they explored a nearby beach. Later, they packed up, ready to go home.

What **2-D** and **3-D shapes** can you see?

In the car, they heard a deep rumble. 'More thunder!' said Omar.

However, it was just Ember snoring.

'She deserves a rest,' Nadia whispered to Omar.

Nadia and Omar giggled.

Nadia's dens

Nadia is reading her den building book. Which **3-D shape** is each of these dens most like?

pyramid **triangular prism** **cuboid**

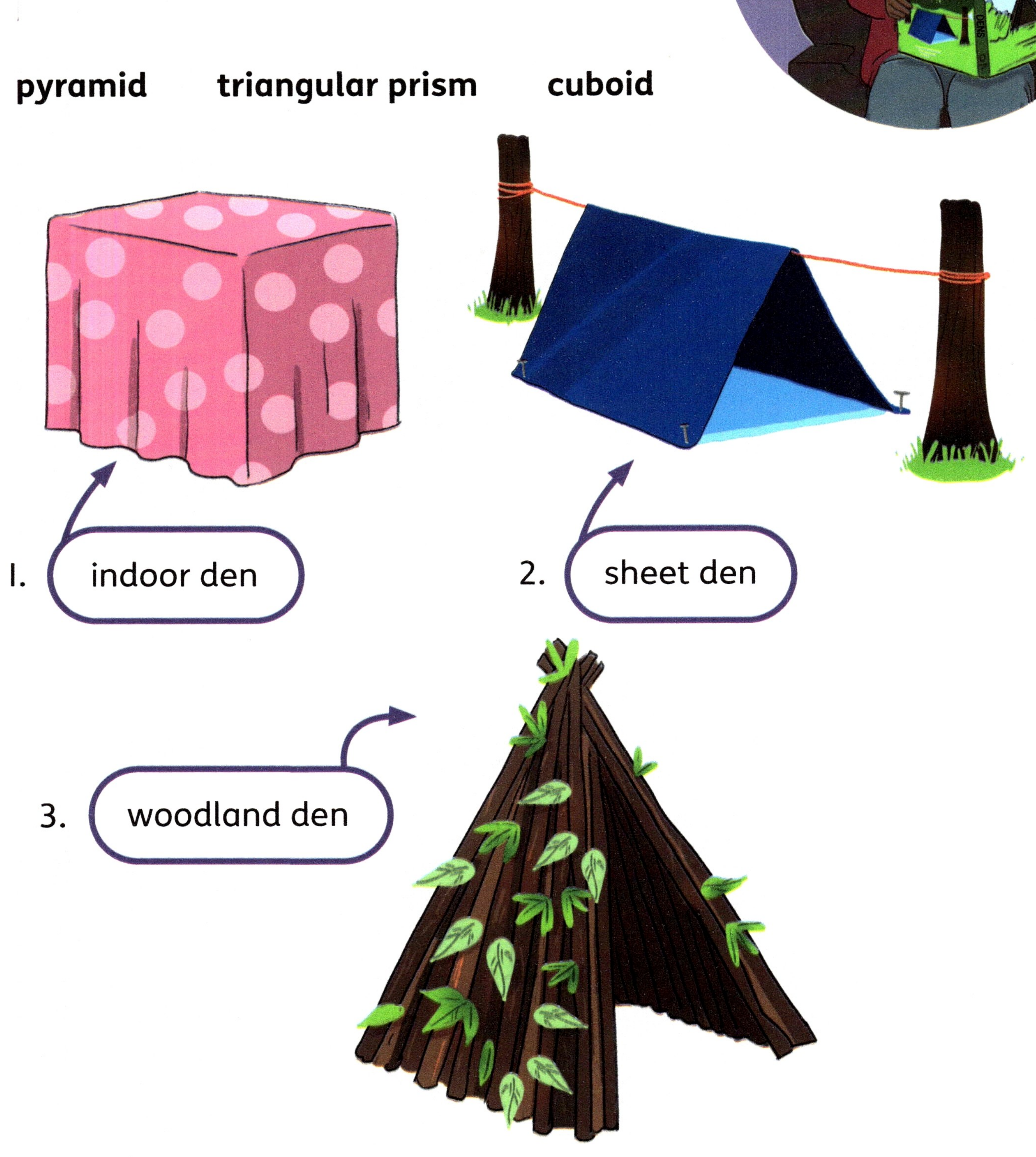

Answers
p13. triangular prism; p24. 1. cuboid, 2. triangular prism, 3. pyramid.